My Christmas Treasury

Cartwheel Books · New York

an imprint of Scholastic Inc.

The Biggest Christmas Tree Ever
Text copyright © 2009 by Steven Kroll.
Illustrations copyright © 2009 by Jeni Bassett.

There Was an Old Lady Who Swallowed a Bell!
Text copyright © 2006 by Lucille Santarelli.
Illustrations copyright © 2006 by Jared D. Lee Studio, Inc.

Christmas Morning
Text copyright © 2004 by Cheryl Ryan.
Illustrations copyright © 2004 by Jenny Mattheson.

ISBN 978-0-545-43647-2

10 9 8 7 6 5 4 3 2 1   12 13 14 15 16

Printed in China 68
This collection first printing, September 2012

New Material Only   Matériaux neufs seulement
Reg. No. 04T-1654309   N° de permis 04T-1654309
Content: Polyurethane Foam   Contenu: Mousse de polyuréthane

Table of Contents

The
Biggest
Christmas Tree
Ever

Written by Steven Kroll
Illustrated by Jeni Bassett

For Kathleen
— S.K.

For Ralph
— J.B.

Once there were two mice who fell in love with the same
Christmas tree, but you had to see it to believe it.

Everyone in Mouseville loved Christmas trees. Every Christmas,
families all over town put up the biggest, most beautiful tree they could find.

But first came Thanksgiving. The day before the celebration, Clayton, the house mouse, took a walk around Mouseville. He knew he should be thinking about giving thanks, but the chill in the air reminded him of Christmas.

"You know what?" he said out loud. "This year I'm going to find the biggest Christmas tree ever!"

Not far away, Clayton's friend Desmond, the field mouse, said exactly the same thing.

That night, Clayton helped his mom and dad, his brother, Andy, and his sister, Trudy, make a special cheese casserole and a nut pie for Thanksgiving dinner.

Over at Desmond's house, Desmond and his brother, Morris, helped Uncle Vernon fix a big pot of vegetable stew and a cheesecake.

Everyone ate much too much. After dinner, Clayton's grandma and grandpa sat in the living room, holding their tummies and grumbling.

Over at Desmond's, the cousins from across the road stretched out on Uncle Vernon's sofa and took a nap.

The following morning, Clayton woke up early. He wanted to be first at Clara's Christmas Tree Farm at the edge of town. That way, he could have his pick of the biggest trees!

Over at Desmond's house, Desmond tumbled out of bed
with the same thought.

Clayton hurried over to Clara's, but it was hard to go very fast. He was still too full of Thanksgiving dinner. By the time he reached the Christmas tree farm, he was out of breath. He looked around. No one else was there.

Moments later, Desmond arrived. He too was full of Thanksgiving dinner. He too had found it hard to hurry. He took a deep breath and stumbled inside.

Clayton wobbled down the rows of trees. Here was a nice one,
but it was much too small. There was another, but it was squat and had
a crooked top. Over there was a third, but it was average height and had
big gaps between the branches.

Struggling down another row, Desmond was having the same problems.

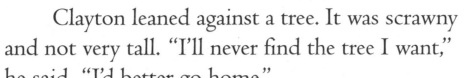

Clayton leaned against a tree. It was scrawny
and not very tall. "I'll never find the tree I want,"
he said. "I'd better go home."

And not far away, squinting at
another tree, Desmond said, "I'll never
find the tree I want. I'd better go home."

When Clayton reached his house,
it was only the middle of the morning.
But he was still full, and he was tired.
He fell back into bed.

When Desmond reached *his*
house, he too went back to bed.

Clayton woke up for lunch and spoke to his dad.

Dad said, "Go out this afternoon. Walk to the far edge of the Christmas tree farm. The biggest trees are there."

When Desmond woke up for lunch, Uncle Vernon told him the same thing.

That afternoon, Clayton went out again. At the very same time, Desmond did too.

Clayton walked to the far edge of the Christmas tree farm. He looked at one big tree after another, but none of them looked like the biggest Christmas tree ever.

Down another path, Desmond was having the same bad luck.

Starting to lose hope, Clayton peered around a very thick trunk. Desmond peered around the same thick trunk. They bumped heads and fell down.

"I bet you're looking for the biggest Christmas tree ever!" said Clayton.

"I bet *you're* looking for the biggest Christmas tree ever!" said Desmond.

"Why don't we find it together?" said Clayton.

"No one said we couldn't," said Desmond.

They set out through the rows of trees. They looked and looked until it was almost dark.

Just as they were ready to give up, there it was: a Christmas tree so big and so tall, it reached the sky!

"How will we cut it down?" Clayton asked. "It's much too big for the two of us."

"Where will we put it?" Desmond added. "It won't fit in your house or mine."

Clayton and Desmond smiled.

"Our families will help us," they said together.

And that is what happened. Clayton's dad and Uncle Vernon came out with their axes, and with the help of Clayton and Desmond, they chopped down the giant tree.

Both families called on friends and relations, and together they loaded the tree onto a hundred red wagons and pulled it to Clayton's front yard. There they decorated it with the most wondrous ornaments and colored lights . . .

. . . and on Christmas Eve, with all of Mouseville celebrating around it, the biggest Christmas tree ever lit up the entire hillside.

Clayton and Desmond shared a high five.

"We did it!" said Clayton.

"All of us together!" said Desmond.

THERE WAS AN OLD LADY WHO SWALLOWED A BELL!

Written by Lucille Colandro
Illustrated by Jared Lee

For Marietta and Mia,
who love Christmas
— L.C.

To Ginger Estepp,
longtime dedicated associate
— J.L.

There was an old lady who swallowed a bell.
How it jingled and jangled and tickled, as well!
I don't know why she swallowed a bell.
I wish she'd tell.

There was an old lady who swallowed some bows.
Soft as the snow, were those velvety bows.

38

She swallowed the bows to tie up the bell
that jingled and jangled and tickled, as well!

I don't know why she swallowed a bell.
I wish she'd tell.

There was an old lady who swallowed some gifts.
It gave her a lift to swallow the gifts.

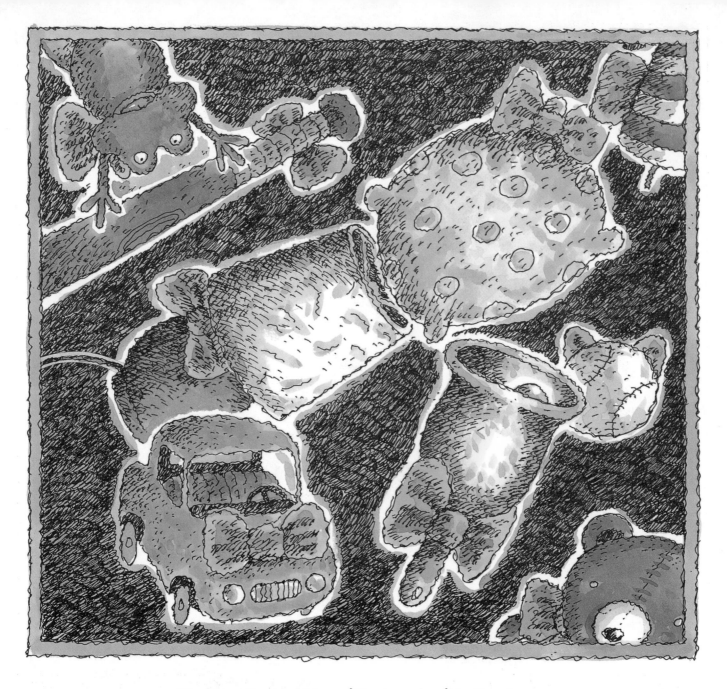

She swallowed the gifts to go with the bows.
She swallowed the bows to tie up the bell
that jingled and jangled and tickled, as well!
I don't know why she swallowed a bell. I wish she'd tell.

42

There was an old lady who swallowed a sack.
It was easy to pack — a very big sack.

43

She swallowed the sack to hold all the gifts.
She swallowed the gifts to go with the bows.

44

She swallowed the bows to tie up the bell
that jingled and jangled and tickled, as well!
I don't know why she swallowed a bell. I wish she'd tell.

There was an old lady who swallowed a sleigh.
What a ton it weighed, that shiny red sleigh!

She swallowed the sleigh to carry the sack.
She swallowed the sack to hold all the gifts.

She swallowed the gifts to go with the bows.
She swallowed the bows to tie up the bell
that jingled and jangled and tickled, as well!
I don't know why she swallowed a bell.
I wish she'd tell.

There was an old lady who swallowed some reindeer.
They were in full flight gear, those soaring reindeer.

She swallowed the reindeer to steer the sleigh.

She swallowed the sleigh to carry the sack.

54

She swallowed the sack to hold all the gifts.

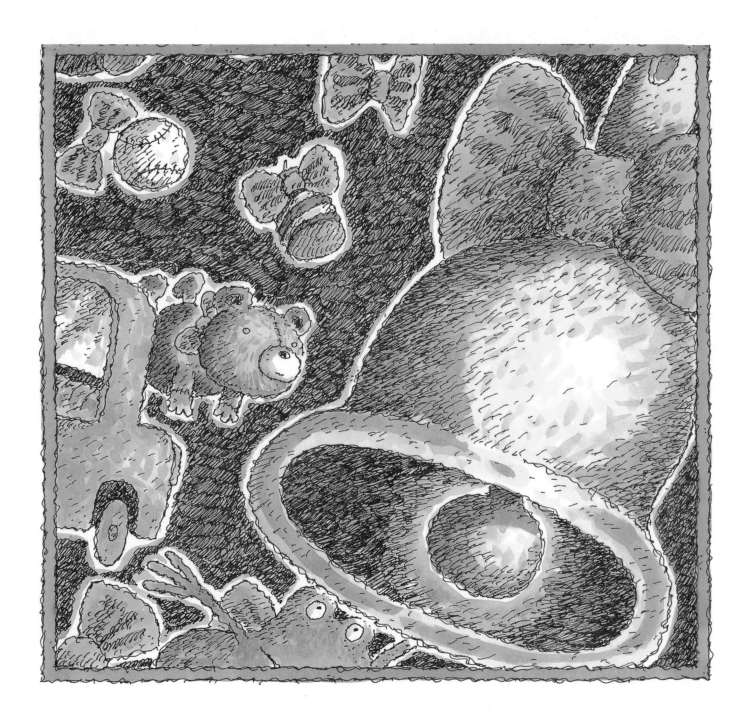

She swallowed the gifts to go with the bows.

She swallowed the bows to tie up the bell
that jingled and jangled and tickled, as well!
I don't know why she swallowed a bell. I wish she'd tell.

Then the old lady needed a treat.
She thought a candy cane would be very sweet.

But when she heard a jolly "Ho! Ho! Ho!"
she knew it was time for her to go.

So she whistled loudly and soon by her side . . .

. . . was Santa Claus waiting for a ride!

Happy holidays to all!

CHRISTMAS
MORNING

Written by Cheryl Ryan

Illustrated by Jenny Mattheson

For Sarah
—C.R.
For all the folks at Christmas Camp
—J.M.

This is the house where the children slept.

This is the snow
that fell on the house
where the children slept.

This is the sleigh
that flew through the snow
that fell on the house
where the children slept.

These are the reindeer
who pulled the sleigh
that flew through the snow
that fell on the house
where the children slept.

These are the reins
covered with bells
that guided the reindeer
who pulled the sleigh
that flew through the snow
that fell on the house
where the children slept.

And this is Saint Nick

who snapped the reins

covered with bells

that guided the reindeer

who pulled the sleigh

that flew through the snow

that fell on the house

where the children slept.

This is the sack filled with toys
flung over the back
of old Saint Nick
who snapped the reins
covered with bells
that guided the reindeer
who pulled the sleigh
that flew through the snow
that fell on the house
where the children slept.

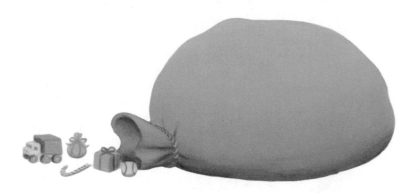

These are the stockings

waiting for toys

to come from the sack

flung over the back

of old Saint Nick

who snapped the reins

covered with bells

that guided the reindeer

who pulled the sleigh

that flew through the snow

that fell on the house

where the children slept.

This is the box

in one of the socks

filled with toys

that came from the sack

flung over the back

of old Saint Nick

who snapped the reins

covered with bells

that guided the reindeer

who pulled the sleigh

that flew through the snow

that fell on the house

where the children slept.

This is the doll
in the box
in one of the socks
filled with toys
that came from the sack
flung over the back
of old Saint Nick
who snapped the reins
covered with bells
that guided the reindeer
who pulled the sleigh
that flew through the snow
that fell on the house
where the children slept.

This is the Rat King
and all of his pack
who frightened the doll
in the box
in one of the socks
filled with toys
that came from the sack
flung over the back
of old Saint Nick
who snapped the reins
covered with bells
that guided the reindeer
who pulled the sleigh
that flew through the snow
that fell on the house
where the children slept.

This is the Nutcracker
who fought the Rat
and all of his pack
who frightened the doll
in the box
in one of the socks
filled with toys
that came from the sack
flung over the back
of old Saint Nick
who snapped the reins
covered with bells
that guided the reindeer
who pulled the sleigh
that flew through the snow
that fell on the house
where the children slept.

This is the train on the track
that carried the Nutcracker
forward and back
to fight the Rat
and all of his pack
who frightened the doll
in the box
in one of the socks
filled with toys
that came from the sack
flung over the back
of old Saint Nick
who snapped the reins
covered with bells
that guided the reindeer
who pulled the sleigh
that flew through the snow
that fell on the house
where the children slept.

These are the children
who wake to find
the train on the track
that carried the Nutcracker
forward and back
to fight the Rat
and all of his pack
who frightened the doll
in the box
in one of the socks
filled with toys

that came from the sack

flung over the back

of old Saint Nick

who snapped the reins

covered with bells

that guided the reindeer

who pulled the sleigh

that flew through the snow

that fell on the house

where the children slept.

And this is Chr